The story of THE SNOW LADY takes place in England—London, perhaps, or Cambridge, or Blackpool. For this reason, some of the words in this story may be unfamiliar to American children. "Biscuits" are cookie-like crackers but without the sweetness of American cookies. Mrs. Dean's "garden" is her backyard. A "cupboard" is a closet, and a "dustbin" is a trash can.

First U.S. edition 1 2 3 4 5 6 7 8 9 10

Library of Congress Cataloging in Publication Data
Hughes, Shirley. The snow lady : a tale of Trotter Street / Shirley Hughes.
p.   cm.   Summary: Sam and Barney build a snow lady that resembles their elderly neighbor, mean Mrs. Dean. ISBN 0-688-09874-6. – ISBN 0-688-09875-4 (lib. bdg.)   [1. Old age–Fiction.]   I. Title.   PZ7.H87395Sn   1990   [E]—dc20
90-53094 CIP AC

A Tale of Trotter Street

The Snow Lady

Shirley Hughes

Lothrop, Lee & Shepard Books
New York

Sam's real name was Samantha, but everyone called her Sam.
Sam's dog was named Micawber, but everyone called him Mick.
Sam and Mick were very fond of each other.

In the mornings, when Sam went to school and Sam's mum and
dad and her big sister, Liz, went to work, Mick stayed at home to
guard the house.

When school was over, Sam walked home with her friend Barney and his dad. As soon as Mick heard Sam's footsteps, he put his front paws on the windowsill and barked a joyful welcome. Sam longed to put him on his lead right away and run off up Trotter Street, with Mick pulling her along and sniffing excitedly at gates and lamp posts. But Mum was still at work and, as usual, she had arranged for Mrs. Dean next door to keep an eye on Sam until everyone else came home.

Mrs. Dean lived alone with her cat, Fluff. Her house was very clean and tidy. The lace curtains were snowy white and the floor was polished like a skating rink. Mrs. Dean welcomed Sam with a glass of milk and two plain biscuits. Sam balanced them on her lap and tried not to drop crumbs while she and Fluff and Mrs. Dean sat side by side on Mrs. Dean's beautiful blue sofa and watched television.

Mick was never allowed into Mrs. Dean's house. He and Fluff got on very badly whenever they met. Sam could hear him howling mournfully next door.

"Whatever has got into that dog?" said Mrs. Dean. She opened her front door and shushed at Mick from the doorstep, but he didn't take a bit of notice. He just went on howling.

Sam and Mick were both glad when they heard Mum's key in the lock. Mrs. Dean's garden was just as neat and tidy as her house. When Mick got in there and started to dig holes searching for imaginary rabbits, or picked a fight with Fluff, Mrs. Dean became very cross.

Mrs. Dean didn't even like Mick to be on the street. Sam and Barney
and the other children often played on Trotter Street after school, and
Mick always joined in. But before long, Mrs. Dean's face would
appear at her window. She would tap sharply on the pane, then put
out her head and say to Sam:

"That dog really ought to be chained up. My poor little Fluff is so frightened she daren't come out."

Or she would say: "Would you mind asking your friends not to sit on my wall?" Or: "A little less noise, dear, please." And that was the end of their game.

But now the weather was getting too cold to play out of doors. One night the water from a leaking drain froze on the pavement outside Sam's house, turning it into a sheet of ice. The Trotter Street children had a great time running up to it as fast as possible and seeing how far they could slide. They hung on to one another and all slid together in a chain. Wheee! It was just like the Winter Olympics! Mick ran alongside, skidding and barking.

Soon Mrs. Dean popped out wearing a shawl over her shoulders. "That's very dangerous," she said. "You might easily break your arms or legs! Do stop at once."

Everyone stopped sliding except Barney. He was at the end of the chain and just kept going. He cannoned into Harvey. Harvey cannoned into Billy, who fell against Mae, who slipped over, pulling Sam and the others with her. There was a terrific pileup.

"I'm glad Mrs. Dean doesn't live next door to us," Barney said later, when he and Sam were drying their feet. "She's always interfering and she hardly ever smiles. She's an old meanie. Mean Mrs. Dean, I call her!"

It was getting near to Christmas. People in Trotter Street were buying Christmas trees and putting up decorations. Mrs. Dean hung a wreath of plastic holly tied with red ribbons on her door.

Everyone admired it except Mick, who took a savage dislike to it. He barked fiercely every time he caught sight of it. Sam had a terrible time trying to drag him past Mrs. Dean's house whenever they went for a walk.

One day Mick got out on his own and worried the ribbon until he got one end of it between his teeth.

Then he pulled the whole thing down and ran off up Trotter Street with the wreath round his neck and the ribbons streaming out behind. Mrs. Dean was very cross indeed. After that, Mick was in bad disgrace.

Sam was pleased when she heard Mrs. Dean telling Mum that she
was planning to spend Christmas with her married son. And sure
enough, on the very day before Christmas Eve, Sam saw her setting
out in a taxi, taking Fluff in a cat basket and a great many parcels.
Hurrah! thought Sam.

Then something even better happened. Out of a slate-gray sky it
began to snow. Big flakes whirled down, covering the pavements
and parked cars of Trotter Street with a soft, white blanket.

Next morning the sun came out and so did Sam and Barney. They decided to build a snowman where the snow lay thickest, between Sam's front gate and Mrs. Dean's. First they piled the snow into a big heap. Mick watched with interest.

Soon there was something that looked like a person with a round head, stick arms, and stones for eyes, nose, and mouth.

"Let's give him a top hat and a scarf and a pipe," said Barney.

"Then he'll be a real snowman!"

Sam and Barney went indoors. Mum was busy, but she said they could pick out some old clothes from the top of the cupboard if they liked.

But Sam and Barney could not find any of the things they wanted, only a lot of hats and dresses belonging to Mum and Liz.

"It'll just have to be a snow lady," Sam decided.

They dressed the snow lady in hat and coat, put a shawl over her shoulders, and hung a handbag on one of her stick arms. She looked very realistic.

"I know who she reminds me of," said Barney. And he moved the stones so that her mouth turned down instead of up.

He searched in the snow for some more small stones and arranged them where the snow lady's feet would have been. The words stood out clearly:

Sam giggled. The snow lady really did look rather like Mrs. Dean. But Barney had not finished. He rearranged the D in Dean to make an M. Then the stones read:

Mrs Mean

"Lucky she's away," said Sam, "How awful it would be if she could see it!" Then they heard Mum calling and ran indoors, taking Mick with them.

The rest of the day was so busy and exciting that Sam and Barney forgot all about the snow lady.

Late that night, long after Barney had wished them all a Happy Christmas and gone home to hang up his stocking, Sam was too excited to sleep. She got up, drew the curtains back a little, and looked out at the street. Everything looked white and Christmassy, but big black clouds were scudding across the moon. When she caught sight of the snow lady, still standing there all alone, it gave her quite a shock.

Then Sam saw a taxi draw up. Out stepped Mrs. Dean! The driver unloaded Fluff and the luggage and helped her into the house. Mrs. Dean walked right past the snow lady without even glancing at her. But she'll see her tomorrow when it's light, thought Sam. It will hurt her feelings. And on Christmas Day too!

Sam decided she must go out at once and kick away the stones that spelled out the snow lady's name. She would take off the clothes too.

It was *terribly important!*

Sam crept quietly downstairs and began to put on her coat over her pajamas. But Mick heard her and came running into the hall, barking and making a great fuss.

Mum put her head round the living room door. "Whatever are you doing, Sam? You can't possibly go out at this time of night!" And she packed Sam firmly off upstairs. "The sooner you're asleep, the sooner Christmas will be here," she said, kissing her good night.

   Still Sam could not get to sleep. She felt too awful about Mrs. Dean.
When she did fall asleep, her dreams were full of excited visions of
Mick, Fluff, and the snow lady and lots of Christmas parcels all tied
up with yards and yards of red ribbon. Mrs. Dean was inside one
of the parcels. She jumped out and then they were all running and
running....But it was not feet that Sam heard in her sleep.
It was rain.

When Sam woke up it was still dark. Christmas morning! And yes, the stocking at the foot of her bed was full of exciting surprises. But Sam did not put on her light yet.

Instead she ran to the window. She could hardly see out because rivulets of water were streaming down the pane. Below, in the street, Sam could just see the snow lady. She seemed to have slumped back against the gatepost and all around her lay a puddle of water.

Then a great, warm hope leapt up inside Sam. She skipped back into bed and began to open her stocking.

As soon as Christmas Day
had begun properly and all
the family had kissed one
another and given their presents,
Sam slipped out through the
front door.

It had stopped raining.
The snow lady had
collapsed altogether.
Her hat had fallen over
her face, and her clothes
were limp and dripping.

Sam kicked the stones and scattered
them about. Then she picked up
the snow lady's clothes
and pushed them
into the dustbin.

She was only just in time. Mrs. Dean's front door opened and out came Mrs. Dean, dressed for church.

Mum hurried to their doorstep to call out "Merry Christmas, Mrs. Dean! I didn't know you'd come back!"

"A merry Christmas to you all, Mrs. Robinson. My son and his wife have flu and couldn't have me to stay after all," said Mrs. Dean.

"Then of course you must come and have Christmas dinner with us," Mum said at once.

"Why, thank you! That's very kind," said Mrs. Dean. And her face melted.

Sam stood right in front of what was left of the snow lady. The name that had stood out so clearly in the snow was now just a jumble of stones lying in a pool of water. Sam shuffled them about with her feet, just in case.

"I expect you wish the snow had lasted longer," Mrs. Dean said to Sam.

"Oh no, I don't mind a bit, really," said Sam. And she gave Mrs. Dean one of her biggest, most Christmassy smiles.

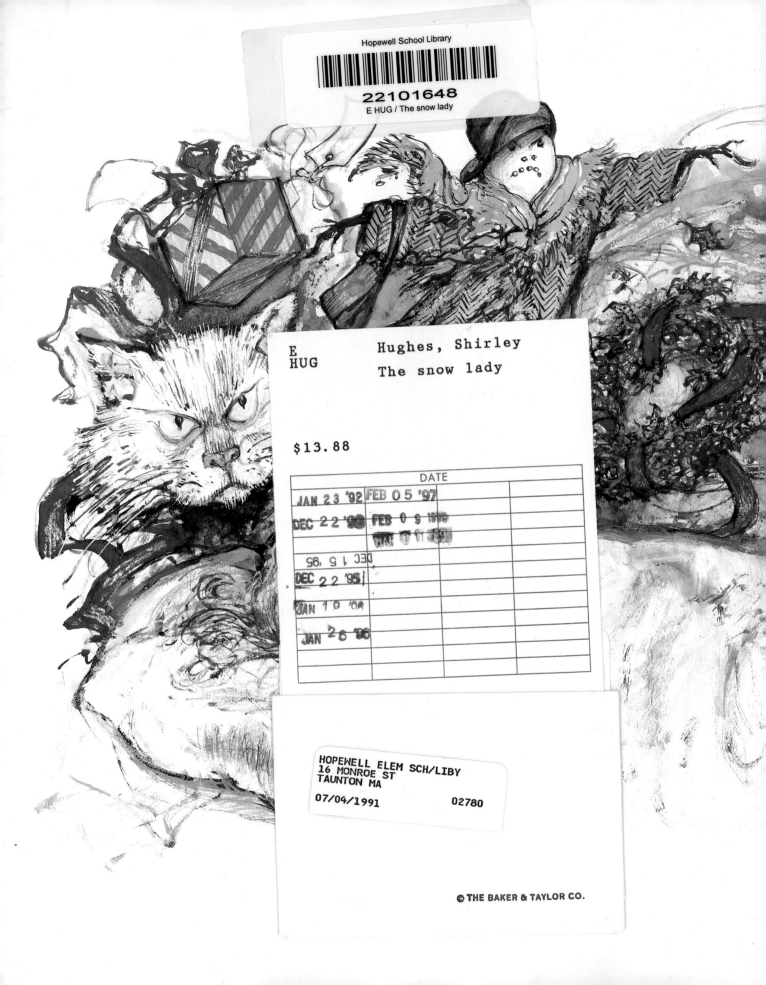

E
HUG

Hughes, Shirley

The snow lady

$13.88

DATE			
JAN 23 '92	FEB 0 5 '97		
DEC 22 '92	FEB 0 9 1999		
	MAR 0 11 1991		
DEC 15 '95			
DEC 2 2 '95			
JAN 1 0 '06			
JAN 2 6 '00			

© THE BAKER & TAYLOR CO.